The double whammy.

All at once I was feeling very strange—light-headed, faint, woozy. That pounding pulse in my nose was getting stronger by the minute. And yes, Drover had been correct in thinking that my nose was beginning to swell just a bit.

Quite a lot, actually.

All at once I was seeing parts of my face that I'd never noticed before, and I seemed to be looking at them with eyes that were growing smaller and smaller, almost as though they were . . . well, swelling shut, so to speak.

The sting of a bumblebee will do that, cause a guy's face to swell up, and two stings in the same general area will increase the swelling by two or three times.

The Case of the
Double Bumblebee Sting

John R. Erickson

Illustrations by Gerald L. Holmes

Puffin Books

PUFFIN BOOKS
Published by the Penguin Group
Penguin Putnam Books for Young Readers,
345 Hudson Street, New York, New York 10014, U.S.A.
Penguin Books Ltd,
27 Wrights Lane, London W8 5TZ, England
Penguin Books Australia Ltd,
Ringwood, Victoria, Australia
Penguin Books Canada Ltd,
10 Alcorn Avenue, Toronto, Ontario, Canada M4V 3B2
Penguin Books (N.Z.) Ltd,
182-190 Wairau Road, Auckland 10, New Zealand

Penguin Books Ltd, Registered Offices:
Harmondsworth, Middlesex, England

First published in the United States of America
by Maverick Books, Gulf Publishing Company, 1994
Published by Puffin Books, a member of
Penguin Putnam Books for Young Readers, 1999

10

LIBRARY OF CONGRESS CATALOGING-IN-PUBLICATION DATA
Erickson, John R., date
The case of the double bumblebee sting / John R. Erickson ;
illustrations by Gerald L. Holmes.
p. cm.
Previously published: Houston, Tex. : Gulf Pub., c1994.
(Hank the Cowdog ; #22)
Summary: Hank the cowdog suffers from a dreaded double
bumblebee sting-or is it something much worse?
ISBN: 978-0-14-130398-7
[1. Dogs Fiction. 2. Ranch life—West (U.S.) Fiction. 3. West (U.S.) Fiction.
4. Humorous stories.] I. Holmes, Gerald L., ill. II. Title.
III. Series: Erickson, John R., date Hank the Cowdog ; #22
[PZ7.E72556Cad 1999] [Fic]—dc21 99-19580 CIP

Hank the Cowdog® is a registered trademark of John R. Erickson.

Printed in the United States of America

To Mary Dykema, my mother-in-law,
in appreciation for her many years of
love and support

CONTENTS

Chapter One First Report of the _____ **1**

Chapter Two Tricked by Pete but Not for Long **11**

Chapter Three Pete's a Cheat **20**

Chapter Four A Severe Double
Bumblebee Sting **28**

Chapter Five Sally May Rushes to My Rescue **37**

Chapter Six Okay, Maybe It Was
a Rattlesnake **47**

Chapter Seven Molly Eats Bugs **56**

Chapter Eight Sally May's Secret Crinimal
Record **67**

Chapter Nine Who Needs Buzzards at
a Time Like This? **76**

Chapter Ten Sally May Really Cares, After All **85**

Chapter Eleven Hiccups Overwhelm Her
Compassion **95**

Chapter Twelve History Seems to Repeat Itself,
Doesn't It? **104**

First Report of the _____

It's me again, Hank the Cowdog. It was morning. It was early summer. Slim and Loper were about to leave the ranch for three days to help a friend with his spring branding.

Little did they know, and even littler did I know, that within minutes I would be attacked and bitten by a . . .

Maybe I shouldn't say. It might frighten the kids, and you know how I am about these kids. I don't mind giving 'em a little thrill, but I sure would hate to scare 'em too badly.

So I don't dare mention that I was bitten on the nose by a rat . . . tell you what. For the time bean, we'll just leave it at that and say that I was bitten on the nose by a rat. A big rat.

That shouldn't scare the kids too badly. I mean, everybody knows that rats bite but they don't have poison fangs or stingers. In the meantime, let's see if we can get the little kids into bed, the ones who might be terribly scared if they knew the truth of the matter.

(See, the whatever-it-was that bit me turned out to be quite a bit worse than a rat. Mum's the word.)

So let me set the scenery. Ranch headquarters.

Early morning. Birds chirping and chattering in the big elm trees, mostly blackbirds and starlings and sparrows and those other birds whose names I don't know. I'm not a bird dog.

Swallows. There were several swallows darting around.

And baldheaded peckerwoods, did I mention them? They tap on trees with their beaks. That would give me a headache.

Where was I? Oh yes. Loper's pickup was parked beside the gas tanks. He'd already hooked up the gooseneck trailer and was filling the pickup with gas.

I noticed a certain edge of tension in the air, which is common around here when someone is trying to meet a deadline or get away for a trip. Loper had been looking forward to this trip for a long time, and no doubt he was running behind schedule.

It happens every time.

Slim arrived in his pickup and pulled up beside the gas tanks. He shut off the motor and gave Loper a grin. "Mornin'. How's it going?"

Loper was not wearing a happy face. "Typical. The phone started ringing at seven o'clock. The pressure pump tripped the circuit breaker again. That's the third time in two days. Alfred spilled a full glass of milk at breakfast. It went in my lap and I had to change pants.

"I can't find my good heeling rope. The stock trailer had a flat tire. The pickup was out of gas. I walked into the bathroom to brush my teeth and caught Molly scrubbing the pot with my toothbrush.

"Just a typical day. We're running thirty minutes late and quite a few dollars short, and you need to saddle both our horses. Then, unless lightning strikes, we might be ready to leave."

Slim got out of the pickup and headed for the saddle lot in that slow walk of his. Loper watched him for a moment and shook his head. "That's the slowest human being I ever met. I'd like to see him in a burning house some time. I'll bet he'd walk just like *that*.

"Hey!" he yelled at Slim. "Hurry up, first chance you get! If we don't get on the road, they'll have the first pasture gathered." Slim lifted one hand in the air and continued slouching along at exactly the same pace. Loper grumbled and muttered. "Slowest human I ever saw."

There didn't seem to be much excitement at the gas tanks, so I made my way up the hill to the yard gate. Drover followed. It was morning, after all, and Loper had mentioned something about "breakfast."

4

Over the years, I had noticed that breakfast scraps most often occurred in the morning, after breakfast, and that was definitely worth checking out.

We have two good reasons for checking out the scrap situation. The first is that scraps are delicious, especially breakfast scraps which might include juicy fatty ends of bacon. The second reason is that we dogs feel some obligation to . . .

How can I put this so that it doesn't sound tacky? We dogs recognize that Pete the Barncat gets very little exercise and, therefore, should not be eating certain foods, particularly those that are high in . . . well, fat and juice, such as juicy fatty ends of bacon.

Pete is such a natural glutton that he can't impose discipline upon his eating patterns and he needs friends to, uh, help him. We accept that as part of our job, helping Pete choose only those food groups that are good for his health, such as corncobs, brussels sprouts, and burnt toast.

I'm told that burnt toast is the best thing in the world for cats to eat—makes their coat shine and keeps 'em trim and thin.

Ho! Guess who was sitting beside the yard gate—grinning, staring at us dogs with weird eyes, and waiting to gorge himself on scraps that would make him fat and ugly.

Fatter and uglier, that is.

Pete.

I went lumbering up to him. Without actually troubling himself to move, he winced as though he expected to be stepped on or smacked by my tail—which all at once seemed a real good idea, so somehow they happened. I stepped on him and bopped him across the nose with my tail, tee hee.

He crouched low on the ground and flattened his ears and glared at me. "Well, well. I believe Hankie the Blunder Dog has just arrived."

"Yeah, and me too," said Drover.

"Yes, and aren't we lucky."

I gave him a worldly sneer. "You got that right, Kitty. I hope we're not too late to save you from making a total hog of yourself."

I began sniffing the ground to check for bacon scent. In the course of doing this, my nose came very close to *his* nose, so what did he do? He cranked up that police siren yowl of his.

I froze. My tail stiffened. Our eyes met.

"You seem to be yowling at me, Kitty. What does this mean?"

"It means that you seem to be intruding into my space. Cats need space."

"Oh yeah? Then why don't you fly to the moon? I hear there's plenty of space up there."

Drover broke up on that. "I get it! There's lots of space in outer space, tee hee hee hee. That's a good one, Hank, you really got him with that one."

"Thanks, Drover. It just kind of popped out of my mouth. I guess we can score a big one for the dogs, huh?"

"Yeah, and now we're ahead, one to nothing."

I turned back to the cat. "Now, what were you saying? Oh yes, you had just begun yowling at me and I don't like that."

"I have to yowl, Hankie, otherwise you wouldn't know that you had intruded into my space. You do that a lot, and every time you invade my space, I

7

seem to get stepped on and hit by your tail."

"No kidding? You know, Pete, that almost breaks my heart—almost, but not quite. If you don't want to get stepped on, quit lurking around the gate and trying to hog all the scraps. You'll find plenty of space up at the machine shed. Go up there. We'll even let you have some of our dog kernels."

"They hurt my teeth."

"Oh well, big deal!"

"Cats don't eat dog food."

"Woooo! Bigger deal!"

Drover got another chuckle out of that one. "Nice shot, Hank, nice shot. That makes two for us."

Kitty-Kitty wasn't amused. "And besides, I saw a rattlesnake up there at daylight."

That got my attention. "What? You saw a rattle-snake around the machine shed? I assume that you killed it."

"Well, no, not really. That's more of a dog-job than a cat-job."

I gave him a stern glare. "It's a job for whom-soever finds the snake, Kitty. Rattlesnake bites are not good for little children. Maybe you didn't know that, or maybe you don't care."

"Oh, I care, Hankie. Children are precious—when they're far away and not making noise."

"Well, if they're so precious, then maybe you

ought to make an effort to protect them from deadly and dangerous creatures. Is that asking too much of a cat?"

He licked his paw. "Well, Hankie, I thought of doing something, but then the snake crawled into a pipe and that was the end of it."

I couldn't believe my ears. "Oh yeah, sure, that's the end of it—until one of the kids goes up there and gets bitten!" I turned to Drover. "Drover, I can't believe this."

He was looking at the clouds. "What?"

"I said, I can't believe this."

"I'll be derned. I guess I can't believe it either."

"Do you know what it is that we're not believing?"

"Well . . . not really. I guess my mind wandered."

"Then pay attention. This cat said he saw a rattlesnake in front of the machine shed."

Pete shook his head. "On the west side of the machine shed, Hankie."

"Just as I suspected, on the west side of the shed, near that pile of welding iron and pipe." I turned back to Drover. "This cat saw a deadly rattlesnake this morning, but instead of taking care of the situation and making the place safe for children, he sat there and watched the snake crawl into a pipe. Can you believe that?"

9

"Well . . . I guess I'm supposed to say no."

"Of course you're supposed to say no, because that was a cowardly and chickenhearted thing for him to do, and we can't believe he did it."

"Oh. Okay. I can't believe it."

I whirled back to the cat. "There, you see? Drover can't believe it either. We're both shocked and outraged. You should be ashamed of yourself, Pete."

The cat gave me a haughty smirk. "Oh really? If you're so shocked and outraged, then maybe you ought to do something about it yourself."

"Oh yeah? Well, as a matter of fact, Kitty, that's exactly what I had in mind. Come on, Drover, we've got some business to take care of at the machine shed!"

And so it was that we left the cat in the rubble of his own shameful behavior and went into combat against the deadly rattle . . . the deadly rat. Big rat.

(Hurry and get those kids to bed.)

CHAPTER TWO

Tricked by Pete but Not for Long

~~~~~~

We had gone only a few steps when Drover said, "What's the business?"

I glared at the runt. "We've got a rattlesnake to kill, you brick. What do you think we've been talking about?"

His eyes blanked out, and suddenly he began to limp. "Boy, I'd love to help, Hank, but all at once this old leg just went out on me. Oh, my leg!"

"Never mind the leg. Stay behind me and stand by for some serious combat."

"The pain's terrible!"

To no one's surprise, I was the first to reach the Staging Area in front of the machine shed. Drover and his so-called limp had fallen behind and I had to wait for him to catch up.

11

"Hurry up, Drover. We haven't a minute to spare. This could turn out to be a very serious affair."

"Yeah, I know, and that's the kind that really sets off this leg. I haven't felt pain like this in years."

"Spare me the details."

At last, he joined me at the Staging Area. I studied the Target Zone, an area dominated by medium-to-tall weeds and various hunks of pipe, angle iron, channel iron, and so forth. Collectively, we referred to this material as "welding scraps," for the simple reason that Slim and Loper used it for their welding jobs.

If you want to know why their welding jobs always look junky, it's because they draw their raw material from a pile of junk. And also, they're not such great welders.

Where was I? Staging Area. Combat. Drover and I were fixing to go into deadly combat against an enormous rattlesnake that had been terrorizing the entire ranch and threatening to bite and eat all the little children.

Well, you know where I stand on the Children Issue. Early in my career, I took a Solemn Cowdog Oath to protect and defend innocent little children against all manner of monsters and crawling things, and the fact that this snake had been reported to be twelve feet long and as big around as an inner tube, capable of swallowing children whole and armed with huge fangs and poison that was so vehement that a single drop could kill a charging rinoserus . . . rhinoserous . . . a charging buffalo—all that didn't bother me in the least.

Okay, it bothered me some. A little bit. I've never been fond of snakes, especially rattlesnakes, and maybe I'm scared of 'em, but in this old life, what matters is not what you're scared of, but what you do about being scared.

And it was at that point that I began thinking, "Aw, what the heck, one little snake isn't going to hurt anything." But that was a cowardly thought and I swept it out of my mind immediately. If Drover had known that I was even the least bit afraid, there's no telling what might have happened.

He might have had a blowout on all four legs at once and been crippled for life. We couldn't risk that. He was enough of a nuisance with one bad leg, and the thought of listening to him moan and groan about FOUR was more than I could bear.

So I summoned all my courage and faced the difficult task that awaited me.

"Drover, I'll go first in what we refer to as 'the first wave.'"

"Yeah, and I'll stay here and wave good-bye."

"No, you'll come in the second wave and watch the rear."

"Yeah, and if you're not the lead dog, the view never changes."

"Exactly. You'll guard the rear and the left flank. Do you know what to do if you hear a rattlesnake?"

"Oh, you bet."

"What?"

"Run like a striped ape."

"No, that's exactly wrong. You freeze, hold your position, and try to get a fix on his position. Is that clear?"

"This leg's killing me."

"I understand that you're in pain, Drover, but just remember that disgrace is the worst pain of all."

"But you never know until you try."

I curled my lip at him. "Take my word for it, Drover, and don't even think about retreating from the field of battle until I give the signal. Is that clear?"

"I hope I can stand the pain!"

"You'll find a way, Drover, because at this very moment, even as we speak, your conscience is talking to you."

"It is?"

"Yes, and what it's saying is that if you run off and leave me alone on the field of battle, I will make hamburger meat out of your worthless carcass. Now, let's move out."

And with those touching words, I turned toward the west, took a deep breath of air, lifted my head to a stern angle, narrowed my eyes, and marched off to war.

"Oh boy, this leg is even worse than I thought!"

I tried to ignore the noise behind me and concentrate on every weed and shadow in the Combat Zone, behind any one of which might lurk the huge and deadly rattlesnake. I took one step, and then another.

And another. And another. And then five more. And then . . .

Suddenly there was a blur of motion in the corner of my periphery, a rapid blur of motion. I froze. Drover ran into me.

"Oops."

"Stop that! Didn't you hear me say halt?"

"Not really."

"Well, I didn't say halt, but even more important was the fact that I halted, and when I halt, you halt! And stop running into me when I'm tense and alert. Do you understand that?"

"I guess so. Did you see something?"

"Affirmative. I saw something, but it wasn't a snake."

"Oh good! What was it?"

"A cottontail rabbit. He jumped into that four-inch pipe over there. In other words . . ."

Suddenly the pieces of the puzzle began falling into place. I shot a glance down to the yard gate. Sally May was there in her housecoat, scraping my morning scraps off a plate and giving them all to . . .

"Drover, we've been duped."

"We have?"

"Yes, we have. We've been duped by the cat who sent us up here on a fool's errand."

"You mean . . ."

"Exactly. He sent us up here to look for a snake that doesn't exist."

"Oh, I'm so glad!"

"But you won't be so glad, Drover, that Pete is getting all the breakfast scraps, including the juicy fatty ends of bacon we're so fond of."

"Oh darn. I'm not so glad about that."

"Just as I predicted. Well, we have no choice but to go streaking back to the yard gate and give Kitty-Kitty the pounding he so richly deserves. Are you ready for that kind of combat?"

"Well, let me think here." He rolled his eyes and studied the clouds. "I'm so glad the snake turned out to be a rabbit that I can't feel sad or mad."

"Pete lied, Drover, that's why we're mad."

"Yeah, but that was the best lie I ever heard."

"All lies are bad, especially when they cost us our breakfast scraps. You should be outraged."

He grinned at me. "Yeah, but I'm not. I'm the happiest dog in the whole world."

"In that case, I have no choice but to pull rank, slap an injunction on you, and force you to shut up." I slapped him on the bohunkus. "There's the injunction."

"Thanks, Hank. I can stand the junk as long as there's not a snake in it."

"The junk is in your brain, Drover."

"No, it's right over there in the weeds."

"An injunction has nothing to do with junk. It has to do with . . . you've got me so confused, I don't know what we're talking about."

"Rabbits."

"Yes, of course. Rabbits are an excellent source of entertainment for ranch dogs and they never bite. Any more questions about rabbits?"

"Yeah, just one. How come Pete got all the scraps?"

I blinked my eyes, cut them from side to side,

and tried to shake the vapors out of my head. "Drover, have you ever felt that you might be going insane?"

"No, but I sure wonder about the rest of the world. It's a pretty crazy world."

"Yes, and you account for 90 percent of it. Now hush, don't say one more word!"

"Okay."

"That's better. Let's move out."

And with that, we went streaking down to the yard gate to claim our true and rightful share of the scraps.

CHAPTER THREE

Pete's a Cheat

The lightning dash down to the yard gate went a long way toward clearing my head. Talking with Drover had just about wrecked my mind. He has this incredible ability to take a normal conversation and turn it into mush and confusion.

I never met anyone just like him. Thank goodness. Two Drovers in the same world at the same time would . . . I don't know what it would do, but it would be crazy.

Trees would start growing upside down.

Birds would fly backward.

I'd be counting the number of pink elephants dancing on the head of a pin.

Drover is a weird little dog, and I don't know

how he keeps drawing me into meaningless conversations.

Where was I? My brains were scrambled, is where I was. Oh yes, the lightning dash down to the yard gate. It saved me from the Black Hole of Drover's meaningless conversation.

When I reached the gate, Pete had his tail stuck straight up in the air. He was purring and chewing on a juicy fatty end of bacon. He turned his head ever so slightly and grinned at me.

The entire left side of my lips snurled into a carl, exposing huge fangs that were ready to . . . on the other hand, Sally May was standing on the other side of the fence. Her arms were crossed. She held a big wooden spoon in her right hand. Her eyes were pointed at me like . . . I don't know, two cannonballs.

Laser beams.

Rifle bullets.

I, uh, wagged my tail and gave her a friendly smile, as if to say, "Oh . . . well, good morning, Sally May. What a pleasant surprise, meeting you here with the, uh, cat. Your kitty."

The sounds of Pete slurping over the juicy fatty ends of bacon reached my ears. They leaped up to Full Alert Position—my ears did, not the juicy fatty ends of bacon. My ears leaped upward and my eyes darted to the stupid, greedy cat.

A growl began to rumble in the deepest caverns of my throat, which sort of exposed my true thoughts on the subject of Kitty-Kitty. Up until that moment, I think I had fooled Sally May into believing that I had merely come to observe.

And, of course, to wish her a good morning. Which was true. I had, in fact, wanted to wish her the very best and most sincere good morning, because . . . well, she's a fine lady and she's often in charge of distributing scraps and . . . well, being kind and thoughtful in the morning is right and proper.

But then that growl came ripping out of my . . . hey, I didn't intend to growl. It just slipped out, honest, and gosh, I guess she took it all wrong, thought that I had come to beat up her snotty little . . .

A joke, that's all it was, just a harmless joke. I mean, Pete and I joked around all the time. That growl meant nothing, almost nothing at all.

Pete's smacking filled my ears and I could see him grinning up at me. He was doing it just to inflame me. I knew that, and because I understood his shabby little game, I . . . the growl grew even louder and I found my guidance systems locking onto Target Kitty.

He would pay for this!

Sally May spoke. "Don't you dare! Don't you even think what you're thinking."

What . . . I . . . but . . . how had she known what I was thinking, read my most private thoughts? Oh yes, the growl. That had blown my cover.

Okay, so I stopped growling, wagged my tail, and turned my sweetest, most innocent face toward her. Here was your basic, carefree ranch dog, happy to be alive and just delighted to see his master's wife.

It took so *little* to bring meaning into my life, just a little love and affection, a smile, a kind word here and there, a few tiny morsels of breakfast bacon, and—I found my gaze pulled back to her greedy glutton of a stupid cat and . . .

Oh boy, there was that growl again. It seemed to have a mind of its own and I couldn't control it. There I was, doing Sincere Dog, and that growl just wrecked it.

"I'm sorry, Hank, but you weren't here when I put out the scraps."

What! I'd been . . . Pete had . . .

"If you want scraps, you have to be here."

Yeah, but . . . hey, her sniveling, scheming cat had . . .

"Pete was waiting here at the gate like a good kitty."

Oh yeah, right! And he'd lied and cheated, and then he'd cheated and lied!

I turned back to the cat. "Wipe that grin off your face, Pete, or I'll wipe you all over this ranch!"

He grinned. "The bacon's delicious, Hankie."

"I'm sure it is, but you lied about the snake."

"No, he was there, Hankie, honest. I saw him with my own two eyes, and he even buzzed at me."

"It was a rabbit, Pete, and you know it."

"Whatever you want to think, Hankie, but the bacon is wonderful. I just hope I can hold it all."

The growl returned again, even louder this time, and I was about to drop a bomb right in the middle of . . .

"Hank, stop that! Leave the cat alone."

Leave the cat . . . but he . . . I . . .

"Now go on. Next time, if you want some scraps, come when I call." She leaned forward and looked directly into my eyes. "And maybe, if you're a good dog, I'll give you some. Maybe. Now scat."

Okay, fine. I could take a hint. I could scat. A few measly scraps meant nothing to me, and just to prove how mature I could be about such a trivial matter, I turned to leave and whispered to the cat, "You'll pay for this."

You know what he did? He stuck out his tongue and crossed his eyes! I paused for a moment, hop-

ing that Sally May had seen it and would understand at last that Pete had been the cause of the
entire misunderstanding.

But no. Her gaze was still locked on me. Her
eyes were always locked on ME. She never saw
anything Mister Perfect Kitty did wrong, but there
was plenty of it and . . . phooey.

I didn't care. At least I had won a moral victory
and had proved once again that . . . something. I
had proved something very important and I had
won a moral victory, and I marched back up to the
machine shed with my held head high.

Head held high.

Drover followed me. "It's too bad we missed the
scraps."

"Yes, Drover, but it's too badder that Pete had
to cheat to get them. At least we're not cheaters."

"Yeah, and we still have a rabbit to chase."

I stopped and stared at him. "You know, you're
right. We do have a rabbit to chase."

"I was just fixing to say that."

"And don't you see what this means, Drover?
Chasing rabbits is much more wholesome and mean-
ingful than sitting around and eating fatty bacon.
Ha! Let Pete get fat eating bacon. We'll go chase rabbits and contribute something to this world."

"Yeah, and I hope there's not a snake around."

I couldn't help chuckling. "Don't worry, son. That snake business was just a filament of Pete's imagination, another of his sneaky tricks. I can assure you that if anything bites us this morning, it will be a rabbit, not a snake."

"Oh good."

"Come on. Let's loosen up and have some fun, forget about Pete and scraps and injustice, and just experience the savage joy of being a dog."

"Yeah, it's wonderful."

"It truly is. Now, study your lessons on how to flush a rabbit out of a piece of pipe." I marched over to the joint of six-inch casing where I had last observed the alleged rabbit. "Pay close attention, Drover. The first thing we do is . . ."

"That's the wrong pipe."

"What?"

"The rabbit went in that pipe over there. I think."

"No, he went into this pipe here. I saw him. This is the correct pipe. We always begin with the correct pipe, otherwise . . . what? What would happen if we began with the wrong pipe?"

"Well . . ." He rolled his eyes around. ". . . let's see. There might be a rattlesnake inside it?"

"Ha, ha. No, Drover. That's close, but not quite right. If we chose the wrong pipe, it would be *empty,* in the sense that it would contain nothing."

"I'll be derned. Did that pipe just buzz?"

"This one? No, not at all. You see, this pipe contains a cottontail rabbit, Drover. These little creatures have been known to squeak on a few rare occasions, but mostly they are silent. And no, rabbits do not buzz."

"Yeah, but . . ."

"Rattlesnakes buzz. Rabbits do not."

"That's what I was thinking."

"And this pipe contains a rabbit. Therefore, by simple logic, we see that it did not buzz."

"I thought I heard a buzz."

"It's probably coming from inside your head, Drover. Empty space sometimes generates a buzzing sound."

"I guess that's what it was."

"Now, observe and take note. The first thing we do to flush out a rabbit is to stick our nose inside the pipe, like this." I crouched down and stuck my nose into the pipe. "Then we . . ."

HISS, BUZZ, WHOOSH!!

Huh?

Something had . . . suddenly I felt a . . .

It was probably just a bumblebee.

They live in pipes, you know.

And they sting.

CHAPTER FOUR

A Severe Double
Bumblebee Sting

I went to Full Reverse on all engines and backed my nose out of the pipe. It was beginning to sting and burn.

My nose, not the pipe. Pipes don't burn.

"Drover, I need to ask you a personal question."

"Oh, okay. Ask me anything. I just hope I know the answer."

I glanced over both shoulders and lowered my voice. "This conversation must be held in strictest confidence. I don't want it to be blabbed all over the ranch, in other words."

"Sure, Hank. I'm no blabber."

"Great. I was hoping you'd say that. Drover, do you see anything on my nose—such as a single red mark that might indicate the sting of a bumblebee?"

He twisted his head and studied the soft leathery portion of my nose. "Well, let's see here. Nope, I sure don't."

"Hmmm. That's odd. I could have sworn that something stung me on the nose. In fact, I'm pretty sure something did, which would account for this burning sensation. But you don't see a red mark?"

"Nope, no red mark."

"That's strange, even odd. Because you see, Drover, I feel a pulse pounding inside my nose,

almost as though it were beginning to swell up."

"I'll be derned. I don't feel a thing."

"Yes, well, you wouldn't feel a thing, Drover. You see, if my nose were stung by a bumblebee, you wouldn't feel it."

"Oh, okay."

"I would feel it, but you wouldn't."

"I've got it now."

"And you don't see a red mark on my nose? Are you sure?"

He squinted at my nose. "No, I sure don't see a red mark."

"Hmmmm. That's very strange, Drover, because . . . something is happening to my nose."

"No, I see *two* red marks, but not one."

I stared at him. "What did you just say?"

"Me? I said . . . well, let me think here. I can't remember."

"Did you say something about *two red marks* on the end of my nose?"

"Well, let's see. Yes, I might have said that, sure might, but that's not what we were looking for, so I didn't want to bring it up, I guess." All at once his eyes widened. His ears jumped and his mouth fell open. "*Two red marks!* Oh my gosh, Hank, you don't reckon you were . . ."

"Hush! I know what you're fixing to say, and

don't say it." I cut my eyes from side to side. My data banks whirred and clicked. My nose throbbed. "Two red marks, Drover? Are you sure? Count them again."

"Okay. Let's see. One. Two."

"One more time, Drover, just to be sure. You might be seeing double. You might have miscounted. It happens all the time. And let me remind you that we're looking for the telltale signs of a bumblebee sting, which would be *one red mark on the nose.*"

"Okay, here I go. One . . . oh my gosh, Hank, there's another one . . . two! There's two little drops of blood on your nose, and you don't suppose . . ."

"Hush! We're not looking for drops of blood, you moron! Bumblebee stings don't draw blood. We're looking for one small inflamed red area, that's all. For the last time, do you see it?"

"Well, let me check it again . . . no, I don't see it."

"Fine. Great. That means I was mistaken and nuffing hes heppened to may nothe."

He stared at me and twisted his head around. "Gosh, you're sure talking funny all of a sudden."

"Mo, you wong, Bovuh. I'm mot talking fummy. Thomething must be wong wiff you ee-uhs."

"My what?"

"You ee-uhs."

"My what?"

I put my nose in his face and raised my voice. "YOU EE-UHS! Those things om you het dat you use to heeuh wiff!"

"Oh my gosh, Hank, all at once I can't understand what you're saying, and I think your face is swelling up, and maybe that's why you're talking funny. And Hank, do you know what this might mean?"

"Yeth, of cose I thoo. It meanth that I wath sthung on the nothe by two bimblebeeth, not one."

He rolled his eyes around. "Well, that's not what I was thinking."

"I don watt to heeuh what you are tinkink, Bovuh, because there wath not a rittlesnake in the pipe. It wath two bimblebeeth, pewiod!"

"Well, okay, whatever you think. I can live with that if you can."

"I wiss you wooden pudd it dat way."

"What?"

"I thed, I wiss . . . I tink I bettuh go thee Thally May. Thumping's wong wiff my nothe."

All at once I was feeling very strange—light-headed, faint, woozy. That pounding pulse in my nose was getting stronger by the minute. And yes, Drover had been correct in thinking that my nose was beginning to swell just a bit.

Quite a lot, actually.

All at once I was seeing parts of my face that I'd never noticed before, and I seemed to be looking at them with eyes that were growing smaller and smaller, almost as though they were ... well, swelling shut, so to speak.

The sting of a bumblebee will do that, cause a guy's face to swell up, and two stings in the same general area will increase the swelling by two or three times.

Yes sir, we had definitely taken two direct hits on the nose by an angry bumble ... and yes, I had a strong feeling that Sally May should be informed that her Head of Ranch Security had ...

See, some dogs are allergic to the sting of a bumblebee and that can cause even more swelling of the injured part than ... obviously, I had a slight allergy to bumblebee poison and ...

Staggering? As I made my way down to the yard gate, I found myself staggering. Walking sideways. That's one of the main symptoms of a bumblebee sting, makes a guy walk crooked, and that sure checked out. I was walking crooked.

And foaming at the mouth? Yes, it's common knowledge that bumblebee stings will cause a dog to, well, foam at the mouth. And that checked out too.

What we had here was a classic case of Severe Double Bubble . . . Severe Double Bumblebee Sting on the nose, and were you aware that bumblebees often build their nests in old abandoned pipes? Yes, it happens all the time. Very common.

Sally May had knelt down and was pulling some dandelions out of her yard. Pete lay in the grass beside her, purring like a little chainsaw, twitching the end of his tail, and getting fatter and lazier by the minute.

He heard me coming and opened his eyes. The longer he looked, the wider they grew. Then a smirk leaped across his mouth. Then he started laughing.

"Why, Hankie! Have you been chewing on the air hose? I think your face has been inflated. And oooo! Two little puncture wounds on the end of your nose! I told you there was a rattlesnake up there, didn't I?"

"Thut up, kett. It wath two bimblebeeth, and I haff nothing to thay to you. My bithnith ith wiff Thally May."

Pete shook his head and sighed. "Well, now you've done it, Hankie. Next time, maybe you'll listen to what I tell you. I tried to warn you, but you're too stubborn to listen."

I tried to think of a stinging reply, but all I

could think about was the stinging in my nose. It was hurting and throbbing, don't you see, and all I could manage to say was, "Thut up, kett."

I waited for Sally May to notice my condition, which seemed to be growing more serious by the moment. I mean, the thought had even occurred to me that we might need to make a little trip to town to see the veterinarian.

Double Bumblebee Syndrome can be very serious. Some dogs actually die from it.

I was no fan of the local vet or any other vet for that matter, and I sure wasn't the kind of dog who wanted to rush into town over the slightest little wound or sniffle, but hey, this thing was beginning to . . .

Drooling? Hmmm, it appeared that I was drooling from the, uh, mouth. Couldn't stop it. It was a little embarrassing, and of course, Drover noticed it right away.

"Oh my gosh, Hank, are you drooling?"

I glared at him through my rapidly shrinking eyeholes. "Of coss I'm dwooing, you dunth! What do you espet fwom a seveeoo case of Dibble Bimble-bee Sting?"

"Well, I don't know. I just thought you'd want to know."

"I did not went to know, and I'll think you not

to make a mockawee out of my injuwee!"

At that very moment, I heard footsteps coming up behind me. I turned and saw Slim and Loper approaching from the south. No doubt, they had finished loading their horses and gear, and were ready to leave the ranch.

My serious medical condition would change all that, of course. I hated to ruin their plans. I knew how much they had been looking forward to this big week of roundups and branding, but what could I do?

I gave my tail a sorrowful wag and held my rapidly expanding face at an angle where they could . . .

CHAPTER FIVE

Sally May Rushes to My Rescue

Huh?
They didn't even notice! I mean, they walked right past me, and Slim even stepped on my tail!

"Get out of the road, pooch."

I couldn't believe my . . . how could he . . . I dragged my swollen, suffering body a full eight inches to the north and thus escaped being trampled by my so-called friend.

Loper leaned an elbow on the gate and spoke to his wife. "Well, I guess we're ready to leave, hon. I know everything will be fine, but if you have any problems, you can catch us at headquarters around dark. I left the phone number."

"Well," she stood up, "I hope you boys have a

37

good time, and I hope you'll be careful with those horses. I worry about you."

Loper removed his hat and pulled her into a hug. "Bye, sweet. Tell the kids their daddy loves 'em a whole bunch."

"I will, and they'll miss . . ." She froze. Suddenly it appeared that her eyes had locked in on ME, in my miserable, wretched condition.

Shall we describe my miserable, wretched condition? My nose was throbbing, my entire face and head had swollen up like an inner tube, and it was hanging very low upon my neck. I was staring out at the world with wooden eyes that had almost swelled shut. And I was drooling.

I couldn't control the stupid drooling.

At last, someone had noticed, and it was about time.

Sally May let out a gasp. "My stars, look at your dog!"

All eyes turned to me. I whapped my tail and tried to smile, which wasn't very successful since my face had turned into a balloon. Instead of smiling I drooled a bit more.

Sally May was the first to find her voice. "What on earth has happened to that dog? He looks . . . deformed. And he's drooling!"

Slim and Loper traded glances. Loper rolled his

eyes, shook his head, and turned away. "Geemanee crickets! Of all the times to . . . Hank, you dumb-bell!"

Dumbbell! Me? Well, I . . . how . . . what . . .

Slim shifted a toothpick to the other side of his mouth. "I'd say that Hank found himself a rattle-snake, is what I'd guess. Every ranch mutt finds one sooner or later."

No, it was a bumblebee. Two bumblebees, actually.

Sally May's eyes went from Slim to Loper to me and back to Slim. "Is it serious? What do people do when their dog gets snakebitten?"

Slim shrugged. "Well, it depends. It makes 'em pretty sick. Usually an old ranch dog'll get over it on his own. He'll lay around in the shade for sev-eral days, foam at the mouth, and won't eat, and he'll get as gant as a coachwhip, but then he'll get over it."

"You don't take them to the vet?"

"Well, some do and some don't, Sally May. See, a lot of times, you don't even know the old dog's been bit. He'll go off by himself and lay under a tree somewheres and he won't come back to the house until he's over it, is what usually happens."

Sally May's eyes returned to me. "But that's not what Hank did. He came to me."

"Yep. I guess he likes you, Sally May."

"How could I be so lucky?" She stood there for a moment, shaking her head and moving her lips. "So! You boys are going off to a three-day roundup and your dog picks this very moment to get himself bitten by a rattlesnake." She turned to Loper. "And what am I supposed to do now? Loper, this is YOUR dog."

Loper had been deep in thought. Now he spoke. "Hon, I hope you understand that I didn't plan it this way."

40

"I understand that, dearest."

"We can't cancel this deal. Jimmy's planned his whole roundup around us. We've got to go, and pretty quick."

Her eyes widened. "And leave me here with this . . . this drooling dog?"

Boy, that hurt. I couldn't help it that I was drooling.

Loper nodded. "I'm afraid so. I hate to do it, but when a man gives his word, he has to stand behind it. If we cancelled out over a sick dog . . . we just can't do that, hon."

"Fine. I understand that. I agree. But what am supposed to do with your dog? I don't even like him!"

That one hurt too.

Loper thought it over. "Well, you could just leave him alone and let nature take its course. Just make sure he has plenty of fresh water. Chances are, he'll get over it."

Sally May heaved a sigh. "Yes, and for the next three days, I'll have to look at the poor beast. And if he died, guess who would feel all the guilt and responsibility."

Loper nodded. "Okay. Maybe you'd better load him up and take him to the vet."

"Load THAT dog into MY clean car, and haul him to town with MY two children?"

"You can take Slim's pickup. It already stinks."

Slim nodded on that. "You bet, that'll be fine, Sally May. You won't hurt that old thang. It's just right for haulin' dogs."

"And my children?"

"Oh sure. They won't hurt it."

"Slim, I'm not worried about IT. I'm worried about THEM!"

"Oh."

"The last time I saw the inside of your pickup, I wanted to go get a smallpox booster."

"Naw, I've cleaned it up since then, Sally May. It ain't bad, really."

"I'll bet. I've seen your cleaning jobs before, Slim Chance. You shovel out the dead rats and call that clean."

"Yes ma'am."

She whirled around and faced Loper. She was wearing a crazy smile on her face. "Well! After ten years of marriage, I can't believe you're doing this to me."

"I know, hon, and I feel bad about it."

"This," she shook a finger in his face, "will cost you. I want the floor fixed in the utility room." Loper nodded. "I want the screen door patched." He nodded. "I want a new faucet for the kitchen sink."

"I'm putty in your hands, hon."

"I want two wheelbarrow-loads of manure spread on my flowerbeds."

Loper swallowed hard. "That's a pretty expensive dog."

"And you'll tend to those jobs the very day you get back, right?"

"I guess you've got us pretty well roped and tied."

"All right, I'll take your dog to town."

He gave her a kiss on the cheek. "You're sweet, and you win the Pioneer Mother Award."

"I'll win the Angry Ranch Wife Award if you don't keep your end of the deal."

"It will be done—not joyfully, but it will be done." Loper turned a glare on me. "Well, I guess we've set a market price for you, Hank. You're worth two loads of manure."

Yes, well, two loads were better than . . . uh, one.

Loper and Slim said their good-byes, tramped down to the pickup, and drove off, pulling the gooseneck trailer with two saddled horses in the back. Sally May watched them and waved until they drove out of sight. Then she looked down at me.

I, uh, felt very uncomfortable all at once, and found myself looking away from . . . she had a fairly icy expression in her eyes, don't you see, and ... well, she and I had this long history of misunderstandings, and now here we were, together and alone, our destinies more or less ...

"Why couldn't you have done this yesterday or last week or any day but today?"

I, uh, didn't have an answer to that, and my nose was throbbing, and I felt rotten.

She looked down at me for a long time. Her eyes began to soften. She came over and knelt down beside me and took my inflated face in her hands. She stroked me on top of the head and rubbed my ears.

"Poor Hank. How can I be mad at you when you look so pitiful? Let me get the children dressed and we'll go to town—in Slim's garbage-can pickup. You stay right here."

Yes, ma'am. I sure didn't have any better plans.

She went into the house. Moments later, I heard bulldozers and dynamite, an indication that Little Alfred was awake. Somehow, the thought of riding all the way into town with his noise and motion didn't make me feel better, so I tried to think of a song that would express the misery of my condition. Here's how it went.

I Was Bitten on the Nose
by a Rattlesnake

I was searching for a bunny in a joint of
    rusted pipe.
I stuck my nose inside it and prepared
    to take a bite.
I loosened up my jaws, unleashed a
    deadly growl...
But something stung me on the nose and
    caused me to howl.
At first I thought the cottontail had done
    this awful thing,
But bunnies do not have the means to
    cause a painful sting.
So common sense prevailed and soon I
    came to see
It couldn't be a bunny but perhaps a
    bumblebee? No.

    I was bitten on the nose by a
        rattlesnake,
    A rattlesnake, a rattlesnake.
    I was bitten on the nose by a
        rattlesnake.
    And now I'm swollen up like a
        poisoned pup.

Now, why would a rattlesnake take refuge
    in a pipe?
I've known these guys forever and they're
    really not the type
To be lurking in a junkyard in the middle
    of the day,
But this one hadn't read the book on
    where he's supposed to stay!
I guess I woke him up in the middle of
    his nap.
He didn't even rattle but gave my nose
    a snap.
There's a moral to this song, in case
    you'd like to use it!
Don't stick your nose into a pipe unless
    you want to lose it!

I was bitten on the nose by a
    rattlesnake,
A rattlesnake, a rattlesnake.
I was bitten on the nose by a
    rattlesnake.
And now I'm swollen up like
    a poisoned pup.

CHAPTER SIX

Okay, Maybe It Was a Rattlesnake

So there you are. The song had allowed me to work through the trauma of my situation and to admit what was becoming more and more obvious:

The thing that had attacked my nose was neither a rabbit nor a bumblebee, but rather, a RATTLESNAKE!

Does that shock you? I'm sorry. Facts are facts, and until something better comes along, we must face the facts and deal with them as though they actually mean something.

To do otherwise would be to dwell forever in the land of fantasy and dreams ... which, come to think of it, doesn't seem all that terrible.

Hmmm. Maybe it really was a bumblebee and ...

Perhaps you thought it was a bumblebee. Or

two bumblebees. Yes, there for a minute or two, I'd embraced that theory myself, but on further analysis and deeper inspection, that theory just hadn't cut bait.

I mean, we had this huge throbbing nose right in front of us which pointed to the Rattlesnake Skinnerio. That kind of nose couldn't come from a mere rabbit bite or a bumblebee sting. It was the work of a *rattlesnake*.

Once again, I'm sorry for wrecking your theory. The fact that it was a pretty stupid theory shouldn't discourage you from proposing other stupid theories in the future. Where would we be without stupid theories?

I don't know.

Ask Drover. He's the expert on stupid theories. In fact, wasn't it Drover who had raised the Bumblebee Theory in the first place? Yes, of course.

At last, the pieces of the puzzle were falling into place, and I made a mental note to lower Drover's daily grade by three points for coming up with that nitwit Bumblebee Theory.

You have to watch him all the time. You never know what kind of bonehead idea he'll come up with next.

Where were we?

Oh yes. The weight of evidence had finally

forced you and Drover to admit . . . and we've covered that already and I hate to repeat myself.

And you know how much I hate to repeat myself.

Rattlesnake bite. And I was one sick puppy, getting sicker by the minute.

At last Sally May came out of the house. Baby Molly was forked upon her left hip and Little Alfred was making bulldozer sounds with his lips. They came out the yard gate and started down to Slim's pickup, which he had left parked near the gas tanks.

Sally May called to me and asked if I could walk. I didn't know, but I saw no harm in trying. I jacked my hind end off the ground.

That's the way a cow gets up, did you know that? It's true, but a horse gets up front-legs first. Just thought I'd throw that in.

I jacked my hind end off the ground, pushed hard on my front legs and raised my south end to the same level. It was then that I noticed that my head and face now weighed in close to a hundred and fifty pounds (the swelling, don't you see), which made it difficult to hold my head at its usual proud angle.

My lower lip was dragging the ground, is where we were, and walking is not easy when your lip has become a road grader blade. But I'm no quitter, and I forced myself to make the long walk down the hill to the pickup.

I'm sure that small minds would have thought that I looked ridiculous, and would have laughed and poked fun at my condition. It didn't seem so funny to me.

At last, I made it to Slim's pickup. Sally May opened the door on the driver's side, looked inside, and gasped.

"How can that man ride in this thing! My trash barrel is cleaner than this!"

She set Molly on the ground and began pulling out . . . well, things: five-buckle overshoes, hay hooks, a yellow slicker, a coffee can full of fence staples, wire pliers, a nylon catch rope, a box of cow pills, jumper cables, a pair of spurs, two calf-pulling chains, and a tuna fish can that had been sitting on the dash.

I don't know what was inside the can but it must have been pretty awful. She looked into it and . . . mercy, crossed her eyes, curled her lip, and threw it as far as she could. Then a shiver passed through her entire body and she said, "Ohhh, nasty bachelors!"

She sprinted back to the house and returned with a roll of paper towels and a spray can of . . .

something. She swabbed the seat with paper towels, wiped the dash and steering wheel, and I was
beginning to wonder if she might consider hurry-
ing up a bit.

I mean, we had an emergency snakebite victim
waiting to be rushed to the hospital, right?

She finished the cleaning, picked up the spray
can, pointed it inside the cab, held it at arm's
length, turned her head away, and filled the cab
with a fog of spray.

She opened both doors and fanned the fog

with a chainsaw manual she had found beneath the seat. When the fog had cleared enough so that we could breathe, she pitched Molly into the seat and tied her down with a seatbelt, and told Alfred to load up.

Then she looked down at me. Her hair seemed a little mussed and she swept a wisp of it out of her eyes. "Come on, Hank, get into the car . . . pickup . . . truck . . . whatever you call this junk-heap. Get up, come on, boy. Jump!"

Jump? Was she serious? Jump, with a two-hundred-pound face? I didn't think so, but I did manage to wag my tail and give her a mournful look.

She heaved a sigh. "I guess I'll have to pick you up and load you. I'll try to be gentle."

She wrapped her arms around my chest and gave a mighty lift and, my goodness, you should have heard the groan! She got me off the ground but maybe that threw her off balance just a little bit, because she staggered two steps backward and we all ended up on the ground, with me on top.

Well, the least I could do was to give her a lick on the face for her effort. I mean, I really appre-ciated . . . I tried to give her a lick of appreciation but, alas, my face was swollen so badly that the old tongue just wasn't working and . . .

I guess I drooled on her. A little bit. My face was very drooly, see, because that's what happens when your face and mouth are swollen up, you can't control the flow of . . .

Well, she didn't like the drool, I guess, and after some kicking and squirming, she made it back to her feet. She tore off five paper towels and wiped her face and arms.

Panting for breath, she turned back to me. "Hank, will you please jump up into the car? Please?"

Okay, I would try, but it wasn't a car. No dog in history had ever managed to load himself into a pickup with a two-hundred-pound face, but for Sally May, I would try.

And by George, it worked. Somehow, against tremendous odds, I dragged myself into the cab and collapsed immediately on the floor. I was worn to a frazzle.

She climbed in behind me and slammed the door. "Alfred, sit down and don't say one word until we get to town. Molly, don't touch anything. This whole pickup is poisonous."

"Mom, I smell bananas," said Alfred.

"It's peaches, dear, peach-scented spray." She stared at the instrument panel. "How do we start this thing?" She spotted the ignition key and turned it. We lurched forward and she let out a scream. "A-a-a-a-a!"

Alfred grinned. "It's a stick shift, Mom. You have to put in the cwutch."

She burned him up with a pair of flaming eyes, then said, "Yes, darling. I know that now."

She took a grip on the steering wheel and plunged her left foot to the ... oof! ... floor. Trouble was that I happened to be down there in the vicinity of the clutch pedal.

"Hank, move!"

Huh? Me? Gee whiz, I thought I'd done pretty well just to load myself into the derned pickup and I didn't know she ...

"MOVE! GET OUT OF THE WAY!!"

Okay, okay. I could take a hint, but it wasn't easy, let me tell you. I crawled and squirmed and managed to drag my wounded self a few inches to the east, enough so that she could push the clutch pedal to the floor.

She pushed it to the floor and started the motor. She seized the gearshift lever in her right hand, pushed it straight up, and popped the clutch. We lurched forward: chug, chug, chug!

"Hank, you're in the way again."

Huh? Me? Hey, I had just moved and ...

"I can't reach the gas pedal. You're going to

have to move out of my way. Alfred, can you get this dog out from under my feet? Hank, go sit on the other side. Go on, boy, be a good dog. Hank, MOVE OVER!"

She seemed to be kicking at me with her foot, a clue that she was pretty serious about getting me moved out from under her business. Okay, fine. I just hadn't realized . . . I had taken some comfort in being close to her, don't you see, and moving around in my condition wasn't all that much fun and . . .

Yes, somehow I summoned up the energy and strength to drag my wounded, swollen carcass around the gearshift lever and move it to the other side of the cab.

I collapsed at Little Alfred's feet and gave the boy a mournful gaze. He laughed.

"You wook funny, Hankie, wiff your face all puffed up."

Thanks, pal. "Funny" didn't even come close to describing how I felt, but I was glad that somebody was able to enjoy my snakebite.

Anything to make the kids happy, I always say.

And so it was that we made our emergency trip into town in Slim's pickup. Little did I know that . . . well, you'll find out soon enough, but only if you keep on reading.

CHAPTER SEVEN

Molly Eats Bugs

We went up the hill in front of the house in first gear, known in the trade as "Grandma Low." By the time we reached the top, Sally May had the motor wound up so tight that it was screaming, yet we were not moving very fast.

It was then that she began to realize that the pickup had four gears, and that she would have to do some shifting. With a grim expression on her face, she took a double grip on the steering wheel, pushed the clutch pedal to the floor, reached for the gearshift lever with her right hand, and pulled it straight down.

The gears began to grind. We coasted to a stop as she continued to search for second gear. At last she found it and popped the clutch. That sent

56

everyone's head snapping back, and the pickup leaped forward.

It was a little rough, but we were on our way to town.

At the mailbox, she turned left onto the county road. She was in third gear by then and probably should have shifted down to second, but she was accustomed to driving an automatic transmission instead of a standard stick shift, and she didn't shift down.

I noticed this, and so did Little Alfred. He even offered some advice. "Hey, Mom, you're s'posed to shift the gears."

"Honey, I'll take care of the driving. I'm the parent and you're the child, and if you don't mind, I'd rather not hear your commentary all the way to town."

"Okay, Mom."

"I know that you're trying to help, but this is not the time or place for that. But thanks, anyway."

"Okay, Mom, but you're s'posed to shift the gears."

"Alfred, hush."

The U-joints clanged, the tappits rattled, the motor wheezed and groaned and jerked, and slowly, very slowly, we pulled away from the mailbox. So far, so good.

We came to the first cattleguard and bounced across it. Little clouds of dust drifted down from the ceiling, and seven crazed miller moths came flying out of the heater vents on the dash.

Have we discussed miller moths? I really dislike them a lot. Or to put it another way, I HATE 'em. I mean, here is a bug that can't even fly in a straight line! They fly in those crazy spirals, bump into things, and somehow they always manage to get into your face.

I have been known to watch them for minutes at a time, and then to snap them right out of the air. Shooting down millers is very satisfying, but not for long because they're covered with this powder, this brown dust that tastes awful.

"He who biteth a miller moth soon spitteth."

Have you ever heard that old saying? Maybe not, because I just made it up, heh heh, and I think it's pretty good. It's definitely true.

I love to blast 'em out of the sky, but the taste that follows is no fun at all. It makes a guy have second thoughts about blasting them out of the sky, is what it does, and this time, in the pickup, I merely observed.

I observed them flying their stupid spirals, bouncing off the windshield and the roof and the window glass; accomplishing absolutely nothing, contributing nothing to the good of the world; buzzing around my face and leaving a trail of miller dust everywhere they went—in other words, being totally worthless.

I watched this with mounting rage and irritation, but chose not to snap them out of the air. Why? Simple. First, my face was much too swollen to be an effective snapping device, and second, I had no wish to repeat the follies of my past. I had already learned my lessons on biting millers: Don't.

Well, Sally May coughed on the dust, fanned the air, and managed to bat two of the millers out the window. "I will never drive this pickup again, never! Alfred, try not to breathe the dust."

"What should I bweeve?"

"I don't know, but try not to breathe the dust. Stick your head out the window until it settles."

He stuck his head out the window. At that same moment, one of the crazed millers landed in Baby Molly's lap. I watched this closely to see what she would do. I had a feeling that she might . . .

Uh-huh, she did. She snatched up the miller in her fat little fist and ate it. She chewed it three times, made a sour face, and spit it out. The miller ended up hanging by a wing on the point of her chin.

I saw the whole thing and had a pretty strong suspicion that Sally May wouldn't approve. I whined and thumped my tail, which succeeded in pulling her eyes away from the road.

When she saw that brown ring of miller dust around her baby daughter's mouth, and the dead bug hanging off her chin, she almost had a stroke and a wreck at the same time.

"Molly, nasty miller, nasty! Spit, spit."

By the time Mom had gotten all the nastiness wiped off of Molly's mouth and chin, the pickup had wandered off the side of the road and into the ditch and was heading toward a big cottonwood tree.

Alfred saw it coming. "Hey, Mom, you're heading for a twee."

Sally May jerked the wheel back to the left and got us back on the road. "Alfred, I saw the tree. I'm not blind."

"Yeah, but you were fixing to have a weck."

"We were NOT fixing to have a wreck, and don't tell your mother how to drive. Molly ate a bug."

Molly laughed and blew bubbles of spit. Alfred gave her a disgusted look.

"Mowee, don't eat bugs. That's dumb."

"Honey, it's not dumb, it's just unsanitary. And take my word for it, you ate plenty of bugs when you were Molly's age." The pickup had begun to stray toward the ditch again and she jerked it back. "Now, let's all sit back and relax and try to enjoy the ride to town, and let Mommy concentrate on her driving."

Hear, hear.

Sally May took a double grip on the wheel, turned her eyes to the road ahead, and let out a big breath of air. We rode in near silence to the main highway.

You may not believe this, but when silence

finally fell over our little group, I began thinking of a song about kids eating bugs. It was a pretty cute song, and it's too bad I don't remember it.

You would have enjoyed it.

Boy, I hate to forget a good song.

Should have written it down, I guess, only dogs don't write.

Wait a minute, hold everything. It just came back to me. It's called "Eating Bugs Is Lots of Fun."

Eating Bugs Is Lots of Fun

I know that some amongst you will more
    than likely think
That eating bugs is yucky, they're ugly
    and they stink.
But stop and reconsider before you make
    a leap.
The bug supply's unlimited, and boy,
    they're really cheap.

Eating bugs is lots of fun,
It won't require a hotdog bun.
Nourishment for everyone.
Eating bugs is lots of fun.

You're s'posed to drink a glass of juice
  before your breakfast meal.
Well, bugs are juicy as can be, the price
  is just a steal.
You'll find no cheaper protein than a
  cricket served for lunch,
And with every bite of cricket, you get
  a pleasant crunch.

  Eating bugs is lots of fun,
  It won't require a hotdog bun.
  Nourishment for everyone.
  Eating bugs is lots of fun.

But here's a few precautions, in planning
  your attack.
Beware of wasps and scorpions 'cause they
  will bite you back.
And earthworms are a special case, they
  have no legs or toes,
And if you try to eat 'em fast, they'll wrap
  around your nose.

  Eating bugs is lots of fun,
  It won't require a hotdog bun.
  Nourishment for everyone.
  Eating bugs is lots of fun.

Bugs are better for you than corndogs on
    a stick.
The only disadvantage is that bugs can
    make you sick.
Don't eat too many june bugs or miller
    moths or flies,
'Cause if you do not chew them up, they'll
    tickle your insides.

Eating bugs is lots of fun,
It won't require a hotdog bun.
Nourishment for everyone.
Eating bugs is lots of fun.

Pretty good song, huh? You bet it was, just full
of important dietary information and good practi-
cal advice. I mean, kids like Molly are going to eat
bugs anyway, so we might as well give 'em some
instructions on how to do it right.

Anyways, where were we? Oh yes, we were in
the pickup, rushing me and my snakebit nose to
the doctor in town. How was I feeling? Very puffy,
I guess you'd say, and not too full of energy. My
highest ambition at that point was to lie down in
a shady place and stare.

And drool. We were still getting a lot of action
in the Drool Department.

Well, we came to the place where the county road runs into the main highway. Sally May stopped at the stop sign, mashed the clutch to the floor, and went looking for first gear. She missed and got third gear instead, and we went clattering and jerking out onto the highway.

A big eighteen-wheeler cattle truck came zooming around us and blew his horn. You know how that irritates me, smart aleck truck drivers blowing their horns and playing big shot on the highway. On a better day, I would have given that guy a barking he never would have remembered . . . a barking he would have remembered and never would have forgotten . . . a stern barking, in other words, but with the swollen face and everything, I had to let him go with a growl.

Sally May heard the growl, and I guess it must have sounded kind of pitiful. She reached down and scratched my ears.

"Poor old Hank. I know you don't feel good. Now that we're on the highway, I'll try to make up some time—if this garbage can of Slim's will hold together."

Boy, I appreciated that. I mean, Sally May and I had had our ups and downs and our little periods of misunderstanding, and the fact that she would exceed the speed limit and go streaking into town just for me . . . well, that meant a lot.

And I was very sorry that the highway patrol-man was waiting over the next hill, but I can't take the blame for that.

CHAPTER EIGHT

Sally May's Secret Crinimal Record

I don't think we had been speeding for very long, but I guess it was long enough.

Alfred was the first to spot the officer's car parked on the side of the road. We had just zoomed over a hill and, bingo, there he was at the bottom. All at once, the roof of his car began flashing blue and red lights, I mean, it looked like a prairie fire up there.

"Uh-oh, Mom. Wooks wike you got nailed."

I noticed that Sally May's eyes rolled so far up in her head that they just sort of vanished for a moment. Kind of scared me, to tell you the truth, but then she snapped out of it, pulled over to the side of the road, and came to a stop.

She left the motor running. Maybe she wasn't

sure it would start again. Good thinking.

She drummed her fingers on the steering wheel and took a deep breath. The officer came walking up to the window, a nice-looking fellow with brown eyes and a round face. On his shirt, he wore a little nameplate that said "Rocha."

"Good morning, ma'am."

Sally May managed a smile. "Good morning, Officer Rocha."

"We've met before on this road, haven't we?"

"Yes, Officer Rocha, we have met before on this road." She took a deep breath of air. "Officer Rocha, this has been a very bad morning for me. My husband's dog was bitten by a rattlesnake . . ."

She pointed to me. I wagged my tail and tried to squeeze up a big smile for the officer but, well, squeezed up some more foam and drool on my mouth.

". . . and I'm trying to rush him to the veterinarian."

"Yes ma'am. I had you clocked at sixty-two coming off that hill."

"And I'm very sorry."

He nodded and smiled. "May I see your driver's license?"

Her eyes went blank for a moment, then darted to the seat beside her. "Officer Rocha, would you

68

believe that I remembered to load the dog and the children . . . but forgot my purse?"

Lines of concern gathered on his brow. "Hmmm. That's not so good." He took down her name, address, and so forth, and wrote it down on a pad. "Does this pickup belong to you, ma'am?"

"No sir, it belongs to our hired hand, and I wish I'd never seen it."

"Did you know the license tag is expired?"

There was a long, throbbing silence. "No, Officer Rocha, I didn't know that."

"Three months ago. And maybe you didn't notice, but the inspection sticker is out of date too."

"I'll kill him."

The officer stepped back and cocked his ear. "I'm guessing that your hired man needs a new muffler."

"Believe me, the next time I see him, he'll get a new muffler."

He returned to the window. "By any chance, are you carrying proof of insurance?"

Sally May leaned across the seat and opened the glove box. It contained one greasy glove, a petrified apple, and three mud dauber nests. She slammed it shut.

"Officer Rocha, who will take care of my children while I'm in prison?"

He got a laugh out of that. And then he started writing out tickets. "Ma'am, I'm going to let you go with three warning tickets, but I'll have to cite you for not carrying your driver's license. Just sign all these on the line."

She slashed her name across the bottom of all four tickets. The officer gave her copies. "When you get your dog fixed, I'd recommend that you not drive this pickup until it's tagged and inspected."

"That, sir, will happen."

"And in Texas, we do require proof of insurance."

"Yes sir."

"Watch the speed, ma'am, and have a good day."

For some reason, she started laughing. "I'm sorry, Officer, but this is one of the worst days of my life."

"Well, I hope it gets better."

He returned to his car. Sally May ground the gears until she found one that would work, and off we went with a chug and a cloud of blue smoke.

There wasn't much conversation on this last leg of the trip. Little Alfred must have sensed that this would be a good time to observe total silence, and so did I. I hardly dared to breathe. Even Molly was quiet.

Sally May, on the other hand, had quite a bit to say, but she said most of it under her breath, where we couldn't hear it. I picked up just enough to know that this was not the day for joking or idle chatter.

At last, we reached the vet clinic over on the east side of town. Doctor Hardy was a pleasant man, but his office made me nervous. It was filled with strange devices and odd smells. I took one look around the place and said, "I'll see you folks back at the ranch," and headed for the door. But he had already closed it.

At that point, I tried to hide beneath a chair, but he and Sally May dragged me out. I had all claws extended and set in the Anchor Position, but the floor was made of slick linoleum and I couldn't get a grip. They put me up on a metal table.

I liked the vet right up to the moment when he came at me with that needle, and at that point I decided to bite him. But somehow he distracted me with smooth talk and ear-scratching, and . . . well, before I knew it, he was finished and I never got around to . . .

Maybe next time, when I felt better.

He told Sally May that I would be swollen for several days and that I should stay in a cool place with plenty of water close by. To which she said, "I hope that doesn't mean in my house."

"Well, that's up to you. The cooler, the better."

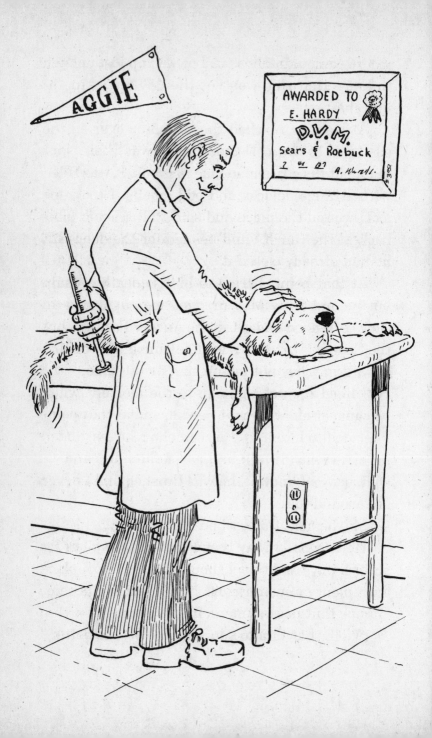

He lifted me off the table and set me on the floor. "The good news on these snakebites is that the dog builds up an immunity. The next time he gets bitten, he won't be so sick."

Sally May's eyes narrowed. "Next time? You don't think he's learned anything from this?"

The doctor laughed. "Oh no, they never learn. Sometimes they go right back to the same place and the same snake and do it all over again, until the snake either moves out or dies from exhaustion. Some of these old ranch dogs get two or three bites every summer, and their owners don't even bother to bring them in."

I could hardly conceal my outrage at this . . . this disgraceful and insulting . . . who or whom did he think he was talking about? Maybe your ordinary ranch mutts went back to the same place and the same snake and got bit again, but hey, I was no ordinary ranch mutt.

I was the Head of Ranch Security, and for his information and for the record, I learned quickly and never forgot any of life's painful lessons.

And there would be no more snakebites for me, thank you, Doctor. And all at once I didn't think he was such a swell guy, spreading lies and phony information, and I had a suspicion that he'd BOUGHT that diploma on his wall from . . .

somewhere. Sears and Roebuck, maybe.

And besides all that, he was an Aggie! And what did an Aggie doctor know about dogs or anything else?

Yes, I was outraged.

He had lost all credulity with me.

Next time, I would just take my doctoring business somewhere else . . . although there wouldn't be a next time.

I should have bitten him when I'd had the chance.

"Dogs never learn." The very idea! I had never been so insulted.

We made the drive home without any major wrecks or incidents with the police department. Oh, we did make one stop—at the fireworks stand on the south end of town, of all places. That didn't make any sense to me until later, and then it made quite a lot of sense. You'll see.

When we got back to headquarters, Sally May got some rags and gunnysacks and made me a little bed in the shade beside the water storage tank. I suppose she figgered that would be the coolest spot for a dog in my condition, although . . .

I, uh, gave her Sad Looks and Slow Wags to remind her that, well, it would probably be quite a bit cooler and nicer inside the house. She had an air-conditioner, don't you see, and while I didn't really approve of air-conditioners for ranch dogs, this was kind of a special case.

I mean, me being sick and everything. Swollen up. Terrible fever. Raging terrible fever.

Okay, maybe I was feeling better after getting the shot from that phony vet, but still, it's foolish to take chances with the Head of Ranch Security, right?

But we didn't succeed in selling that idea to the, uh, lady of the house, so to speak, and I took up residence beside the storage tank and settled into a long and boring period of recoveration.

It was long and boring. Drover came up to keep me company, but that made it only longer and boringer. In spite of all his many flaws, he is a boring dog. At last, he even bored himself and went away.

That left just me and the flies. The flies were terrible. They were driving me nuts. I hate flies. And then . . .

You'll never guess who arrived on the scene. Hint: two big black ugly birds whose presence was not exactly an omen of good fortune.

CHAPTER NINE

Who Needs Buzzards at a Time Like This?

~~~~~~

G ive up? I knew you'd never guess.
Wallace and Junior the Buzzards.

I saw them floating around in the sky above me and hoped they would go away. They didn't. They kept gliding around in circles and dropping closer to the ground with each circle until, with much thrashing of air and flapping of wings, they landed in the elm tree, right above me.

I didn't growl or bark at them (too much trouble with the swollen face and everything) but I did glare daggers at them. What did they do? Well, they stared at me, craning their long skinny necks and twisting their ugly bald heads.

Have you ever been stared at by a couple of hungry buzzards? It's no fun, take my word for it. It does something to a guy's self-confidence. I mean, even if you feel comfortable about who you are, even if you have a strong self-conceit, even if you're fairly sure that you won't end up on their dinner plate, there's just something about their presence that ruins a good day.

How do they stand each other's company? Have you ever wondered about that? I have. I can't imagine spending all day, every day, around a buzzard. How depressing. Maybe that's why Wallace is always in such a bad mood.

However, Wallace didn't seem to be in a bad mood at the moment. He was hopping up and down on the limb and seemed almost beside himself with . . . I don't know. Wild buzzard joy, I suppose.

"Son, this could be it! This could be the moment we've been longing for and waiting for, all these many days! What do you reckon?"

"W-w-well, he h-hasn't m-m-moved, hasn't moved, s-s-so m-maybe h-h-h-h-h-he's . . ."

"Hurry up, son, you talk too slow and here I am, starved down to bones and pinfeathers. Speak up."

"Uh uh, okay. M-m-maybe h-h-h-h-h-h-he's . . ."

"Never mind, Junior, let's move along and cut to the bottom line. What is he, and will he eat?"

"W-w-w-well, l-l-let's s-see."

"Is he a badger? From upstairs, I thought he
was a badger but now I ain't so sure. I could sure
use some badger, yes I could."

"W-w-well, h-his f-f-face is uh-uh-awfully f-f-
fat, awfully fat."

"You're right, son, and most of your badgers
don't have a fat face, so what could he be?"

They both gawked down at me.

"P-p-p-p-pa?"

"What."

"I th-think he j-j-just b-b-b-b-b-blinked his eye."

"No, he never."

"Y-y-yeah, he d-d-did."

"He never, and for very good reason. It's a well-known fact in all parts of this world that dead badgers don't blink."

"Y-y-yeah, b-but h-he m-may not b-b-b-be a b-b-b-b-badger. Badger. Where's the s-s-stripe d-d-down his b-b-back?"

The old man was silent for a moment. "Well, maybe he don't have a stripe down his back, Junior, but are you going to let little details clutter your mind? For you see, Junior, we don't eat the stripe, and I won't turn down a badger just because he don't have one."

"Y-y-yeah, b-but if he d-don't h-have a s-s-s-stripe, h-he can't b-b-be a b-b-b-b-b-b . . . one of those things."

"Badger."

"Y-yeah, a b-b-b-b-b-b-b-b . . ."

"I hear you, I hear you. All right, fine, maybe he ain't a badger, so what do you reckon he is?"

"I d-d-don't know, P-p-pa, but h-he b-b-blinked."

"He did not blink."

"D-d-did too."

Wallace turned to his son, puffed himself up, and bellered, "*He did not blink,* and how can you say such a terrible thing at a time like this! And scoot over, you're a-crowdin' me off of this limb."

"P-p-pa?"

"What!"

"I th-think it's our d-d-doggie f-friend."

Wallace whipped his head around and stared at me. "No, he ain't our doggie friend, in the first place because we don't have no friends amongst the doggies or anything else that's fit to eat, and in the second place, he ain't a doggie. He's a dead badger."

"N-n-no, h-he ain't a b-b-badger, P-pa, and h-h-he ain't d-d-dead t-t-too."

Wallace began jumping up and down on the limb. "Junior, I am your father and I have spoken and you will show some respect to your own flesh and blood, and I'm a-telling you, that right there is a dead badger!"

Junior gave his head a sad shake. "O-okay, f-f-fine. H-he's a d-d-dead b-b-b-b-b-b-b . . ."

"Badger."

"B-b-b-badger."

Wallace studied him for a moment. "Junior, do you really believe that with all your heart and soul, or are you just sayin' it because I said it first, and I want the truth, son?"

"N-n-number T-t-two."

The old man's chin fell down on his feathered

chest. "Junior, you just don't know how much this hurts me. I ask you for the truth, the honest truth, and what do you do? You give it to me!"

"W-w-well? Y-you asked f-f-for it."

"Son, what I was askin' for and pleadin' for from the very bottom of my heart was something dead to eat, and a badger would be just perfect. But no, you've told the truth and denied your pore old daddy the simple joy . . . son, do you really, honestly think it's a dog?"

"Y-yep, I d-d-do."

"And do you really and truly believe he blinked his eyes?"

"Uh-huh."

"This hurts me, Junior, more than I can express, but life is full of hurt."

"Y-y-yep, it is. Y-y-you w-want me to ch-check it out?"

Wallace heaved a sigh. "Check it out, son. If it's bad news, I'll try to hold back the tears."

Junior leaned his neck in my direction and gave me a big buzzard smile—which, in case you haven't seen one at close range, is about the ugliest smile you can imagine.

"H-hello d-down there. Y-y-yoo-hoo."

I gave my enormous swollen head a nod. "Yoo-hoo to you too."

Junior turned to the old man. "S-s-s-see? H-he s-s-said y-y-y-y-yoo-hoo b-back."

"So? That don't mean . . . keep a-checkin' it out, son, he might be on his last leg."

Junior turned back to me. "Is that y-y-you d-d-down there, D-d-d-doggie?"

"Yeth, it ith, Dunior."

He twisted his head from side to side. "M-my g-g-g-goodness, y-you sure are t-t-talking f-funny this m-m-morning."

"Thankth. Tho would you, if you'd been bitten on the nothe by a rittlethnake."

"A w-w-w-what?"

"A rittlethnake."

Wallace chimed in. "A what? What was that? What did he say, son?"

"W-well, s-s-something about r-r-riddles."

"Riddles? Tell him we're busy birds, we ain't got time for playing riddles." Wallace glared down at me. "Play riddles on your own time, dog, we're lookin' for something to eat."

"A rittlethnake, you dumbbell buzzood!"

Junior's eyes grew wide with excitement. "Oh P-p-pa, I've g-g-got it n-now, and y-you'll b-be s-s-so happy!"

"Son, a squashed badger on the highway would make me happy, but what's he talkin' about?"

"A r-r-rattlesnake."

"Okay, fine, where's he at? In depression times, I'll sure take a rattlesnake."

"N-no. Our d-d-doggie f-friend was b-b-bitten on the n-n-n . . . face by a r-r-rattlesnake."

The old man's greedy little eyes popped open and a smile spread across his beak. "Son, at last you have brought joy to my heart! You have made me a happy buzzard!"

"I t-t-told you."

"Yes, you did and you're a fine boy, Junior, a fine boy, and you'll grow up to be a fine buzzard one of these days, a credit to your family and all of buzzardhood!"

Junior grinned and ducked his head. "Th-thanks, P-pa."

"And yes, this dog is our friend, our true friend, and it's a cryin' shame he got snakebit but a dog can't live forever. Eh, how long do you reckon we'll have to wait, son?"

At that point, I'd had about all the company I could stand. I pushed myself up and gave Wallace my most menacing glare.

"Buzz off, buzzood. Skwam. Get wost. Go fwy a kite. I may wook pwetty bad wiff this swowen nothe, but I ain't fixing to be wunch for the wikes of you. So skat, shoo, skwam!"

Wallace gasped. "Son, he just told us to scram. Did you hear that?"

"Y-y-yeah."

"He told us to scram and he's no friend of ours, I can tell you that, and if that's the best he has to offer . . . dog, you have ruined my day, completely ruined my day!"

"Good."

"And this is good-bye, and in parting, I want you to know that you look silly with your face all swole up, and if I looked as goofy and talked as goofy as you, I'd . . . I don't know what I'd do, but Junior, it's time we got airborne and started huntin' grub!"

With that, he pushed himself off the limb and went flapping off in the morning sky. Junior shrugged and grinned down at me.

"W-w-well, w-win a few, l-l-lose a f-few. S-s-sometimes I think P-pa's w-worse than a s-s-snakebite."

"I'll bet. Or even a wingworm."

"B-b-bye, D-d-doggie. I h-hope you g-get b-b-better. Or w-w-w-worse."

"Thee you awound, Dunior."

And away he went, leaving me alone with my handicap.

CHAPTER TEN

Sally May Really Cares, After All

There was one small detail about the location of my sickbed that hadn't occurred to me: Sally May had put it in a spot that she could see from her kitchen window.

Do you realize what this meant? Maybe you don't and maybe I didn't either, but what it meant was that Sally May *cared* about my health, safety, and physical condition, even though she had gone to some lengths to hide her concern.

Consider the evidence in this case. She had not allowed me into the air-conditioned comfort of her house, right? And that was . . . well, I won't say that it was cruel and unfeeling of her. Or heartless. Callous. Cold-blooded.

I'd be the last dog to say anything critical of my

85

master's wife. I know she had her priorities, and keeping her house neat and clean was high on her list—quite a bit higher than my personal health, safety, and well-being.

I understood that. I accepted her just as she was, and I'd be the last dog in the world to suggest that she was, well, cruel and unfeeling, heartless, callous, and cold-blooded.

No, you'd never catch me making critical remarks about the very lady my master had chosen with whom to share his life. With. With whom. But her weird sense of priorities probably struck YOU as being cruel, unfeeling, and so forth, and what YOU think is important.

Yes it is, and if YOU want to say that she had her priorities and sense of values all messed up and backward, there's nothing I can do to stop you. It's a free lunch.

A free ranch, I should say.

Freedom of speech is a precious right.

I'm sorry you feel that way about Sally May, but just between you and me and the gatepost, there's probably more than a germ of truth in what you've pointed out. And you know where I stand on the issue of germs. I'm totally against 'em.

Germs are bad for everyone, and anything that's bad for everyone can't be all good.

And where were we? Sometimes I get started on a thought, usually a deep philosogical point, and I forget whether it's raining or Tuesday. Actually, it was sunny and Monday, and I have no idea what . . . something about Sally May . . . boy, sometimes I . . .

Wait, I've got it. Okay. Here we go.

For a while there, it appeared to YOU, not necessarily to me, it appeared to YOU that Sally May was a cruel and so forth person because she had left the wounded and suffering Head of Ranch Security outside with the flies, buzzards, and boring morons such as Drover.

But what you forgot or never knew or didn't notice was that she was observing me from her kitchen window, an indication that she really did care about me. And no doubt, she saw me in my state of misery—tormented by flies, roasted by the sun's evil rays, racked or wracked by thirst, whichever way you spell it, and last but not leased, gazed upon and mocked by a pair of half-crazed graveyard buzzards.

You thought she was cruel and unfeeling? Had a heart of stone, and we're talking about absolute granite? Well, hang on and stand by for this next piece of news.

No sooner had Doom and Gloom, the buzzards,

departed the scene than Sally May came out of the house, passed through the yard gate, said something nice and kind and totally inappropriate to her stupid cat, hiked up the hill to the storage tank, and looked down at me.

And yes, I did rise to the occasion and did give her the Look of Maximum Woe and Misery. And thumped my tail many times. And summoned up the little groaning sound that I use only on very special occasions.

And by George, it worked!

"All right, Hank McNasty, I surrender. I hung tough on everything but the buzzards, and that was too much, even for me. Why, if someone from the church drove up . . ."

She placed her hands on her hips and leaned down, so that I couldn't possibly miss the, yikes, stern lines on her face.

"If I let you in my house, will you act civilized?"

Oh yes, ma'am.

"Are you capable of being rational and sane and civilized for a few hours?"

Oh yes, ma'am, on my Solemn Cowdog Oath!

She raised a clenched fist. "And buddy, if you barf on my clean floors, if you chew on my sofa, if you wet on my carpet, YOU WILL . . ."

I held my breath, waiting for her to finish that

terrible sentence. What would it be? Marched out-side and shot? Torn to shreds and pieces? Fed to the crows? Barbecued slowly over mesquite coals?

"YOU WILL REGRET IT!"

Whew! That was an acceptable risk. I could go for that.

You bet, she had my Most Solemn Cowdog Oath that I would never, never do any of the so forth, never ever. But if I did, through some freakish act of nature, I would most certainly regret it.

With all my heart.

And soul.

And liver.

Forever.

But of course, the odds against such a thing ever happening were infantassible. Sally May was taking no risk whatsoever, almost no risk at all.

She dropped her cleansed fish, which I was very happy to see because, believe it or not, she had actually punched me in the nose on several occasions, with that very same . . .

Did I say "cleansed fish"? I meant clenched fish.

Cleansed fist.

Clenched fitch.

Her upraised hand contracted upon itself so as to form a deadly weapon, such as a club.

She dropped her cleansed fish and straightened up, much to my relief, and spoke to me in a kinder tone of voice.

"I shouldn't do this. I know what will happen. You can't be trusted. But what's a poor woman to do? God gave me a heart and a conscience." She lifted her eyes toward the sky. "Thank you, Lord . . . I guess." Back to me. "Now, can you walk to the house or do I have to carry you?"

Well, I could have probably . . . that is, being carried sounded pretty good to me, and after all, I was in a weakened, swollen condition, and if it was all the same to her, well, being carried would be fine.

I gave her Very Sad Eyes and Slow Wags, as if to say, "Walking is out of the question, I hate to be such a burden, I really do, but maybe you ought to, uh, carry me, so to speak."

"I don't believe I'm doing this," she said. Then she bent over, wrapped her hands around my chest, picked me up with a loud groan, and began staggering down the hill.

I felt terrible about it.

We made it to the yard gate. There, she set me down, leaned against the gatepost, and gasped for breath.

Between gasps, she said, "How could you weigh so much?"

It was all that poison, no doubt. Rattlesnake poison is very heavy.

"Well, can you walk the rest of the way?"

I, uh, thought that one over—ran my gaze to the back door of the house and calculated the distance involved and . . . no, as much as I hated being a burden and an invalid, my old legs just couldn't carry me that far.

Boy, I hated that.

When she'd caught her breath, she picked me up again and off we went toward the house—she staggering and grunting under her terrible burden, and I with all four legs pointed straight east.

We passed Pete the Greedy Sneaky Barncat. He watched our little procession with a look of purest envy. I gave him a little grin and said, "She loves me more than she loves you, ha ha ha."

Oh, that killed him! Right there in the space of a few seconds, he died a thousand deaths and I lived a thousand lives, all of them happy ever after.

It was one of the greatest moments of my entire career, and the little snot deserved every bit of it for telling me lies about the rattlesnake. See, he'd been the one who had . . .

Well, I couldn't remember every little detail of the morning's tragedy, but I did know that it had

been entirely his fault, because he had . . . something.

Yes, I feasted on his sour look, and it was as sweet as honey in the mouth of my memory.

We left Kitty-Kitty sitting in the ruins of his own shambles, and staggered down the sidewalk to the back door. There, Sally May dropped me again and more or less fainted against the side of the house, once again gasping for breath.

"I'm too old for this. I can't nurse a dog and raise two children at the same time. Hank, I've carried you this far. Do you suppose you could walk the rest of the way?"

I studied on that. I would have done just about anything for Sally May, and boy, you talk about feeling guilty! But no, I sure didn't see any way of doing that.

I mean, I was actually getting weaker by the second.

She caught her breath at last, propped the screen door open with her . . . well, with her fanny, so to speak, picked me up once again, and off we went into the utility room.

I couldn't be blamed for the laundry basket that was parked right in the middle of our road, and no one could have been sorrier than I that she fell into it.

It was nobody's fault, just one of those things that happen.

Little Alfred was standing in the kitchen, dripping a stolen Popsicle on the floor. He witnessed the accident and thought it was funny, the little snipe. And he started laughing.

Sally May didn't think it was so funny. Her finger shot like an arrow toward the boy. "YOU stop dripping on my clean floor, young man, and YOU . . ." This arrow was pointed at, well, me, it seemed. ". . . can walk into the kitchen, because I'm not carrying you another step!"

Okay, okay. Fine. Sure.

I didn't mind walking. It was the least I could do.

No big deal.

But she didn't need to screech at me like that.

Dogs have feelings too.

Clenched fist, that's what it was, not a cleansed fish.

CHAPTER ELEVEN

Hiccups Overwhelm Her Compassion

She made me a pallet on the kitchen floor and issued some stern orders. I was to remain in that portion of the house which had linoleum floors—meaning the kitchen and utility room. I was not allowed under any circumstances to set foot on any of her carpet.

Well, that seemed reasonable enough, and I even understood the basis of her concern. She wanted to keep her carpet nice and clean, right? And some dogs were not as fussy about their personal cleanliness and hygiene as I, right? So she had passed a law that no dogs were allowed beyond the Linoleum Zone.

In other words, the law had not been created just for me, and in fact, Sally May probably realized that she didn't even need a law to govern my behavior.

I understood about carpet—that it needed to be protected from dirty dogs and dumb dogs with no couth or manners. Yes, I had known hundreds of them in my time, and yes, she had good reason to be concerned about what they might do.

I shared her concern 100 percent and knew that, as long as I was inside her house, the carpet would be perfectly safe, even if I happened to stray beyond the Linoleum Zone.

Which I did. Out of sheer boredom. A guy gets tired of seeing the same four walls and counting the spots on the same old linoleum and . . . well, one thing led to another, and I didn't think it would cause any great disaster if I ventured into the living room to check things out.

But, yikes, she seemed pretty serious about enforcing her law, even though it didn't really apply to me, and she more or less insisted that I remain in the kitchen—under her stern gaze.

No problem there. I understood. A lot of these dogs behave like apes and gorillas when you let 'em inside a house, and her law was good, just, and necessary.

And I understood that she had to be consistent. That's the only reason she made me stay on the linoleum, don't you see. If it applied to one dog, it had to apply to all dogs.

She appeared to be working up a batch of wild plums for jelly. She had found a nice thicket of plums several days before, and she and the kids had picked two grocery sacks full. Now she had to wash and sort them, boil them in a big pot, and mash the juice out of them.

It was a big job. I would have been glad to help, but I could see right away that there wasn't much a dog could contribute to the effort.

Now, if she had been cutting up a chicken or preparing a roast or trimming some steaks, I might have been moved to . . . well, show more interest in the proceedings. But plums didn't interest me much.

So I sat on my pallet and watched—stared at her, you might say, through the narrow eye-slits on my swollen face. Now and then, I caught her glancing in my direction. I thought nothing of it at first, until all of a sudden and for no reason that I could see, she whirled around and said, *"Will you stop staring at me?"*

Huh?

I glanced around to see if perhaps she had been addressing someone else in the room. No, we were alone, just the two of us, which meant that she had probably spoken to . . . well, me.

Staring at her? What was I supposed to be doing? I mean, what else could a sick, wounded, swollen dog do in her kitchen but . . . hey, she had forbidden me from slinking off to a dark and private corner of the house, right?

And I wouldn't say that I was *staring at her* anyway. I was watching. Observing. Showing interest in her work. Was that such a terrible crime?

I passed it off as a . . . I don't know. A sudden passion, a mistake in identity, something bizarre. And I continued to watch her, to observe her working on this important project and . . .

And ten minutes later she said it again. *"Would you please stop staring at me?* I'm sorry, Hank, I know you don't feel good, but you look horrible with your face all puffed up and drool dripping off your lips. It bothers me. I don't know why, but it does."

Oh boy. What can you do to please these people? Could I help it if I looked "horrible" or that I was drooling? How good would she have looked if she'd been snakebit on the nose?

You know what she did? She stopped her work and rigged up a screen with two chairs and a sheet. She screened me off so that I couldn't watch her anymore! I was shocked, and yes, it did hurt my feelings.

So, with nothing better to do, I stared at the sheet. This must have gone on for half an hour or so, when ... you won't believe this. I had trouble believing it. It was lousy luck and it wasn't my idea and it just happened.

All at once I started hiccuping.

Hic. Hic. Hic.

Again, I thought nothing of it at first. I mean, everyone hic gets the hiccups now and then—dogs, humans, elephants. It's a normal hic process, and it's not something a guy has any control over. I mean, you hic don't just wish that you could start hiccuping, do you?

Of course not. Who wants to look and sound ridiculous? Not hic me.

It probably had something to do with the snake-bite. The poison, the deadly rattlesnake poison, was attacking my system and causing me to hiccup.

Hic.

See?

Hic.

There's another one.

Well, not in my wildest dreams would I have dreamed that anyone would take offense to my hiccups! Would you have thought so? I mean, here's a sick dog who's been confined to a corner of the kitchen and screened off from hic the rest of the world. He's trying to survive his ordeal and mind his own hic business and . . .

Sally May's face appeared over the top of the sheet, and she said, here's exactly what she said, word for word. She said, "Why are you doing this to me?"

I thumped my tail on the floor. Hic. Doing what to her?

"I'm trying to read a recipe. I'm trying to concentrate. I'm trying to make jelly for my family, because I love them and I want to do something nice for them. But I can't concentrate because you're over here HICKING."

Yes, I realized that, and I had no hic control over the alleged hicking. I was a hic sick dog.

"I've read the same line in the recipe five times: 'Add two tablespoons of hick.' Now, will you please stop that and let me finish this job before I ruin the whole batch?"

Sure, you bet. Anything for the good of the hic. Family.

She went back to work. I stared at the sheet and concentrated extra hard on not hicking. No more hicking for me.

Some dogs are able to use their mental processes to impose order and control over their bodies. Did you know that? Yes, it's a rare gift that some of us have.

What you do is sharpen all your powers of concentration down to a tiny beam of concentrated something or other. Mental energy. Light. The mind shifts from being a lightbulb into being a laser beam. You then direct this powerful beam at the germs or worms or whatever it is that causes hicking.

You burn them up, destroy them, turn them into mere vapor. Poof! They're gone. No more hicking.

You see? It worked.

I couldn't help being proud of myself. I've never been one to boast and brag, but this was pretty impressive.

What? You think the hiccups came back? You think I lost my concentration? Ha. No way. My powers of concentration had proved themselves, and all I had to do was maintain that high level of concentration for a couple of . . .

A flea chose that very moment to bite me on the tail section and . . .

Hic.

What rotten luck. I'd been doing so well, I'd just about had the thing . . .

Hic.

Sally May loomed overhead like a thunderhead cloud.

"I'm sorry, Hank. I wish I were a better person, more patient, kind, and understanding. But I'm not, and you're driving me nuts with that hicking, and you're going back outside. Out! And you walk on your own four legs, mister, because I don't need a trip to the chiropractor."

Okay, fine. If she didn't want me . . . I pried myself off the floor and followed her out the back door. I didn't hic care. Staying outside was no big deal to me, but if I died in the night from exposure to the elements, I hoped everyone would know who had hic.

Caused it.

Passing through the back door, which she held open for me, I spied a nice soft patch of iris flowers, right under her kitchen window. No doubt that's where she . . .

"Hank! Keep walking."

No doubt she wanted me to return to the bed she had hic made for me up by the water well, which was just fine. I'd always wanted to die from snakebite beside a water well. On a pallet of rags.

I climbed the hill and collapsed on my bed. She went back to the house and resumed her work. I could see her face framed in the window, and for the rest of the day, I stared at her, drooled, and

hicked, just to prove that I was a free dog and this was a free ranch and I could hick and drool and stare any time I hic wanted to.

Human compassion is a very strange emotion. It seems to flourish after huge disasters, but let a poor dog get a little case of hiccups and it withers like a vase of hic.

Wildflowers.

Did I survive through the night? You'll soon find out.

CHAPTER TWELVE

History Seems to Repeat Itself, Doesn't It?

No, I didn't perish in the night, in case you were worried, and thanks for worrying. I'm glad somebody was worried about me.

I didn't perish in the night, but I didn't sleep so well either, because of all the stupid hicking. Take my word for it, the worst part of being snakebit isn't the swelling or the pain or the drooling. It's the hiccups.

But I felt much better the next day, and the day after that I had returned to my normal, robust state of health. The swelling had pretty muchly gone down. I could talk like a normal dog, without drooling or sounding goofy.

And, thank goodness, the hiccups had passed—although I don't want to talk much about them, for fear they might . . .

Hic. Return.

See? You have to be very foxy with these ——. I won't even say the word. The point is, they went away and I don't want them back.

Yes, by the third day of my recovery period, the snakebite and all its unpleasant aftereffects had become a distant memory. Had it actually happened to me, or had I merely dreamed the whole thing? Shucks, I felt so good that it didn't matter.

The very best part of feeling good was that I settled the score between me and Kitty-Kitty. You might recall that Pete had . . . well, he'd done something. I couldn't remember exactly what, but it had been serious enough that I'd held a grudge for three days.

And I'm not the kind of dog who goes around holding grudges for three days, even against cats, so that tells you that whatever Pete had done, it had been pretty derned serious.

Around ten o'clock that morning, I spotted him down by the yard gate. No doubt, he had gobbled down all the breakfast goodies and was waiting for someone to deliver the lunch scraps and lay them down between his paws.

Typical cat. Too lazy to walk three steps for his next meal, and we could forget about him catching mice in the feed barn or the machine shed. That required much too much effort, and never mind that catching mice was his mainest job on the ranch.

Your typical cat takes care of himself, fellers, and the rest of the world can go to blazes.

I could see, even at a great distance, that Pete needed a good thrashing. He was just lying there, see, getting fatter and worthlesser by the minute; purring, twitching the end of his tail, and playing with a cricket that had walked past.

We can be sure that Pete hadn't troubled himself to find the cricket. That would have required some effort.

So, feeling wonderful and wishing to settle an old score, I went creeping down to the yard gate on paws that made not a sound. At a distance of two feet from the end of his tail, I paused and initiated the procedure which we call, if you will forgive the heavy-duty technical terms, which we call "Kitty's Wakeup Call."

ROOF, ROOF!

Hiss, reeeeer!

Heh, heh.

I loved it. It was a wonderful sight, watching

Kitty turn wrongside-out and scramble up the nearest tree. It made my whole day. It made my whole week. It made me proud to be a dog.

But only moments later, my ears picked up the sound of an unidentified vehicle approaching headquarters from the north. I put fun and games behind me, switched into Scramble Mode, and went streaking out to intercept the villains who had . . .

Okay, relax. It was Slim and Loper, back from their big roundup adventure. They pulled down to the elm grove just west of the gas tanks, and guess who was the first to arrive on the scene and welcome them home.

Me.

I jumped up on Slim, licked his hand, sniffed out his boots and pant legs, and gave him a Big Howdy and Welcome Home.

"Well, pooch, the last time I seen you, your nose was about the right size to fill up a grease bucket. I guess you came through that tribulation okay."

Oh sure. It was a piece of cake. No big deal at all. In fact, I had almost forgotten about it.

I was the first to greet the returning cowboys, but Little Alfred wasn't far behind. He came flying down the hill and threw himself into Loper's waiting arms. Sally May came next, carrying Baby

Molly on her hip. She gave Loper a big hug and a kiss.

It was kind of a nice scene. Loper held Alfred and Sally May held Molly, and they all hugged each other at the same time, and Sally May said, "Aren't we happy to have Daddy back home with us?"

Then Loper said, "Well, hon, how'd it go?"

Her expression changed. One eyebrow shot up and an odd smile flickered across her mouth. "How'd it go? Where shall I begin?"

And she told the whole story of our trip to town in Slim's pickup. When she came to the part about being stopped by the police officer, Slim and Loper roared with laughter. Sally May didn't roar or laugh, but watched them with that same odd smile.

"Let's just say that leaving me with a snake-bitten dog and a totally illegal pickup was not a noble thing to do." They got another laugh out of that. She let them laugh. "And let's just say that you will both pay dearly for your fun, and you can start the yard work as soon as you put up the horses."

The laughter died. Slim and Loper were suddenly scuffing up dirt with their boots and jingling coins in their pockets.

At that point, I left the gathering and went on with my work. See, that pickup and trailer had been off the ranch for three whole days, and some-body had to trademark all eight of those tires. Otherwise . . .

Well, we didn't know what might happen, but those tires needed to be processed right away.

I was in the midst of that job when little Drover came streaking down the hill from the machine shed.

"Hank, oh my gosh, there you are!"

"That's correct, taking care of ranch business and feeling much better, thank you."

"You're welcome. I mean, good. You do look bet-ter and you sound better too. I was sure worried about you for a while."

"I'll bet. If you were so worried, why don't you pitch in and help me process these tires?"

"Well, okay, I guess I could."

"And then we'll need to do a thorough patrol of ranch headquarters."

"Sure, Hank, but there's something I've got to tell you."

"Oh? It can't wait?"

"No, it's pretty important. You remember that cottontail rabbit you chased the other day?"

I ran that one through my data banks. "Rabbit. Oh yes, just west of the machine shed. He took refuge inside a pipe, as I recall."

"That's the one. Well, he's there again. He's out-side the pipe and *he wiggled his nose at me.*"

I froze. I studied the runt with eyes of purest steel. "A cottontail rabbit wiggled his nose at you?"

"Yes, he sure did, Hank, I saw it with my own eyes."

"Well." I stopped processing tires. "This is very serious, Drover, and I have an idea that we're fix-ing to get ourselves into some combat."

"I knew you'd want to know."

"Nice job, son. You were right." I loosened up the enormous muscles in my soldiers. "Okay, I'll go in the first wave. You bring up the rear and guard our flanks. Come on, let's move out."

And with that, we went streaking through the elm grove, past the gas tanks, up the caliche hill behind the house, past Kitty in the Tree . . .

And of course Kitty had some smart-mouth remark. What was it? Something about snakes. Nothing I needed to hear.

I went zooming up to the machine shed, and sure enough, there was Little Mister Wiggle His Nose, sunning himself on the gravel drive. My plan was to swoop in and cut off his avenue of escape. See, I knew that he'd try to make a dive into one of those pipes in the junk pile and . . .

And you might say that he did, cottontails are

111

very tricky and it's almost impossible to get a clean shot at one, and through trickery and pure luck, he managed to dive into one of the pipes.

That was no big deal to me. I'm the dog who wrote the book on getting sniveling little rabbits out of pipes, and I went right to work.

"Drover, I'll bark on this end of the pipe. You bark on the other end."

"Well, I guess . . . but you know, Hank . . ."

"That is a direct order. Do as you're told."

"Yeah, but what about . . ."

I didn't have time to hear the rest of what he had to say. By that time, I had already set up a furious barrage of barking and had stuck my nose into the . . .

Buzz! Hiss! Swish!

. . . pipe which, hmmm, had obviously been taken over by a, uh, nest of bumblebees. And we needn't go into any more discussion about bumble- bees, other than to say that their sting can be very, uh, painful.

And to say that the veterinarian had been more or less correct—I had indeed built up an immunity to, uh, bumblebee poison, and this experience proved to be quite a bit wess painfoo and unpwessant than the foost one.

Case cwosed.

No, wait. One last detail. That evening when
Slim finished up his chores at headquarters, he
climbed into his old pickup and turned the switch.
It exploded! And we're talking about smoke and
fire and whistles and bangs, and Slim holding his
hat and making a dash for the house.

Pretty derned scary. I saw it all through . . .
well, eyes that were somewhat narrowed by
swelling.

Guess who was waiting at the yard gate, laughing and slapping her knees and watching the whole thing. You won't believe it.

Sally May.

Remember the day we came back from town? Stopped at the fireworks stand? And I'd thought that was odd?

Smoke bombs. She'd bought two smoke bombs and she'd hooked 'em up herself to the spark plugs on Slim's pickup.

I told you Sally May was dangerous.

Case closed.

And it was a bumblebee.

No kidding.

HANK
THE COWDOG®

Have you read all of Hank's adventures?

1 *The Original Adventures of Hank the Cowdog*

2 *The Further Adventures of Hank the Cowdog*

3 *It's a Dog's Life*

4 *Murder in the Middle Pasture*

5 *Faded Love*

6 *Let Sleeping Dogs Lie*

7 *The Curse of the Incredible Priceless Corncob*

8 *The Case of the One-Eyed Killer Stud Horse*

9 *The Case of the Halloween Ghost*

10 *Every Dog Has His Day*

11 *Lost in the Dark Unchanted Forest*

12 *The Case of the Fiddle-Playing Fox*

13 *The Wounded Buzzard on Christmas Eve*

14 *Hank the Cowdog and Monkey Business*

15 *The Case of the Missing Cat*

16 *Lost in the Blinded Blizzard*

17 *The Case of the Car-Barkaholic Dog*

18 *The Case of the Hooking Bull*

19 *The Case of the Midnight Rustler*

20 *The Phantom in the Mirror*

21 *The Case of the Vampire Cat*

22 *The Case of the Double Bumblebee Sting*

23 *Moonlight Madness*

24 *The Case of the Black-Hooded Hangmans*

25 *The Case of the Swirling Killer Tornado*

26 *The Case of the Kidnapped Collie*

27 *The Case of the Night-Stalking Bone Monster*

28 *The Mopwater Files*

29 *The Case of the Vampire Vacuum Sweeper*

30 *The Case of the Haystack Kitties*

31 *The Case of the Vanishing Fishhook*

32 *The Garbage Monster from Outer Space*

33 *The Case of the Measled Cowboy*

34 *Slim's Good-bye*

35 *The Case of the Saddle House Robbery*

36 *The Case of the Raging Rottweiler*

Join Hank the Cowdog's Security Force

Are you a big Hank the Cowdog fan? Then you'll want to join Hank's Security Force. Here is some of the neat stuff you will receive:

Welcome Package
- A Hank paperback of your choice
- Free Hank bookmarks

Eight issues of *The Hank Times* with
- Stories about Hank and his friends
- Lots of great games and puzzles
- Special previews of future books
- Fun contests

More Security Force Benefits
- Special discounts on Hank books and audiotapes
- An original Hank poster (19" x 25") absolutely free
- Unlimited access to Hank's Security Force website at www.hankthecowdog.com

Total value of the Welcome Package and *The Hank Times* is $23.95. However, your two-year membership is **only $8.95** plus $3.00 for shipping and handling.

□ Yes, I want to join Hank's Security Force. Enclosed is $11.95 ($8.95 + $3.00 for shipping and handling) for my **two-year membership**. [Make check payable to Maverick Books.]

Which book would you like to receive in your Welcome Package? Choose from any book in the series.

(#   )   (#   )

FIRST CHOICE   SECOND CHOICE

_____

BOY or GIRL

YOUR NAME   (CIRCLE ONE)

_____

MAILING ADDRESS

_____

CITY   STATE   ZIP

_____

TELEPHONE   BIRTH DATE

_____

E-MAIL

Are you a □ Teacher or □ Librarian?

Send check or money order for $11.95 to:

Hank's Security Force
Maverick Books
P.O. Box 549
Perryton, Texas 79070

DO NOT SEND CASH. NO CREDIT CARDS ACCEPTED.

Allow 4–6 weeks for delivery.

The Hank the Cowdog Security Force, the Welcome Package, and The Hank Times are the sole responsibility of Maverick Books. They are not organized, sponsored, or endorsed by Penguin Putnam Inc., Puffin Books, Viking Children's Books, or their subsidiaries or affiliates.

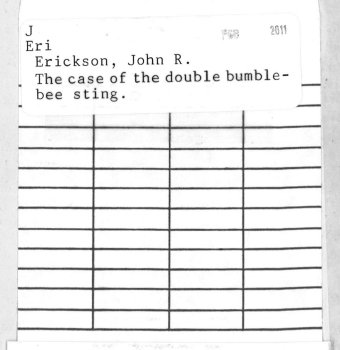